Busy
Critters

Canadian Cataloguing in Publication Data
Tibo, Gilles, 1951-
[Au boulot les animaux! English]
Busy critters
Translation of: Au boulot les animaux!
For children.
ISBN 1-894363-32-9
I. Tremblay, Sylvain. II. Fischman, Sheila. III. Title.
IV. Title: Au boulot les animaux! English.

PS8589.I26A913 1998   jC843'.54   C98-940988-0
PS9589.I26A913 1998
PZ7.T52BBu 1998

© Les éditions Héritage inc. 1998

Publisher: Dominique Payette
English text: Sheila Fischman
Series Editor: Lucie Papineau
Graphic design: Diane Primeau
Colourist: Guy England

Legal Deposit: 3rd Quarter 1998
National Library of Canada
Bibliothèque nationale du Québec

ISBN: 1-894363-32-9

Printed in Canada
10 9 8 7 6 5 4 3

Dominique & Friends
A division of Les Éditions Héritage inc.
Canada: 300 Arran Street, Saint-Lambert, Québec, Canada J4R 1K5
USA: P.O. Box 800, Champlain, New York 12919

Tel.: 1-888-228-1498 • Fax: 1-888-782-1481
E-mail: dominique.friends@editionsheritage.com

We wish to thank the Canada Council for the Arts,
SODEC and the Department of Canadian Heritage for
assisting our publications program.

Some Well-Kept Secrets

Busy Critters

Text by Gilles Tibo
Illustrations by Sylvain Tremblay
English text by Sheila Fischman

For Julie the flea.
For Danielle who's as curly as a…

During the latest International Conference on the Secret Lives of Animals, a child astonished all the specialists by asking: How do animals earn their living?

To answer this disturbing question, we launched a massive worldwide investigation. Now, after years of research, we can confirm that most animals do work: some full-time, others part-time. Before we present the details of our findings, we would like to thank our 12,345 investigators who worked as hard as horses. They've shown themselves to be as stubborn as mules, as quiet as mice, and as curious as monkeys.

The monkey,

who is very good with his hands,
works in a place called "the banana shop."
He uses bananas to repair the trucks, dolls,
teddy bears, and computers that people give him.
Unfortunately, he often works much too fast
and gets all the pieces mixed up.
He needs to be as meticulous as
a little mouse.

The mouse

scampers around busily
in a bakery. The white mouse makes
white bread, the brown mouse, brown bread.
The black mouse has a special job to do.
He makes holes in doughnuts: small holes
for ant-doughnuts and big holes for
hippopotamus-doughnuts.

The hippopotamus

is a lifeguard at the
pool. When he hears someone cry:
"HELP!" he blows his big whistle and jumps
in the water. SPLASH! All the water flies out
of the pool. But every time he does it,
every single time, he has to be very careful
where he lands. Those little rhinoceroses
in the pool have very sharp horns!

The rhinoceros

is a crossing guard outside
the zoo's school. On Monday,
Tuesday, Wednesday, Thursday, and Friday,
he helps the young animals cross the street.
Every morning and every afternoon, he plugs
his ears with cotton. He can't stand the
racket those rabbits make, shouting
and honking their horns whenever
the turtles wind their slow, slow
way across the street.

The turtle

is a letter carrier. Very, very
slowly, she delivers the mail. Letters
that start with "Happy birthday, sweetheart,"
greeting cards, postcards, and presents all
arrive days, weeks, even months late. Everyone
gets impatient. As she makes her way
along with tiny steps, the mailbag on
her back, the turtle wishes she had
long legs like the giraffe.

The giraffe

is an astronomer. With her
friends, she spends hours peering
at the night sky. Through her telescope
she can see the moon, the shooting stars,
and the galaxies. Tonight, the giraffe is very happy.
She is going to be famous all over the planet for
she has made a discovery of astronomical
proportions: the elephant
constellation.

The elephant

drives a big truck. The back of
his truck is loaded with very heavy stones.
Oh, no! A little fly is about to touch down on the
load. Bang! The fly's weight could make the
truck shatter into a thousand pieces!
The elephant holds his breath and dreams
of being as light as a
duck's feather.

The duck

used to be an airplane pilot.
Quack! Quack! Quack! He's just been
fired because every fall at migration time,
he would turn his plane toward the south. With
no concern for his passengers, he makes an
emergency landing, unfolds his beach chair,
puts on a straw hat and stretches out
lazily in the sun, just like a lion.

The lion

is a hairdresser. Snip! Snip! Snip!
With his big scissors he cuts everyone's
hairs. All day long he brushes, washes, dyes
hair, he counts flakes of dandruff,
and massages scalps. And he has another very
special specialty: he loves
to curl sheep.

The sheep

is an alchemist. Tired of being
as meek as a lamb, he spends many long
hours in his laboratory. By mixing different
chemicals he is hoping to discover the secret
that will make him the meanest, the scariest animal
of them all. He is trying to find the magic
formula that will transform him
into a crocodile.

The crocodile,

despite his appearance,
is a dentist with a big heart. Lovingly
and delicately, he fills cavities and
gives advice about oral hygiene. Unfortunately,
whenever he opens his mouth for a
tooth-brushing demonstration, the patient
gets frightened, jumps up and runs away!
Especially the kangaroo!

The kangaroo

works at a daycare centre.
He plays with the children. He makes
them jump for joy, jump rope, jump in the air.
If the children get over-excited, he takes them
for a walk in his pouch, jumping and
whistling lullabies. Nobody is better
at looking after children.

For children,

work is a game. We've seen children fix broken toys. Others play baker, lifeguard, crossing guard, letter carrier, astronomer, truck driver, airplane pilot, hairdresser, alchemist, dentist, baby-sitter. Children, as they play, dream about the jobs they'll have when they grow up.